# Haunted Reflections

## Part 4

Andrew Wilding

To order additional copies of this book, contact:
Martin and Bowman
1-855-921-1348
www.martinandbowman.com

# DEDICATION

I dedicate my books- Scarecrow, Iggy and Wormy, 33 Walking Stones, 4 Souls of Nature to the individuals who deserve it the most.

First I would like to thank the Heavenly Father, Jehovah for giving the gift to write fantasies such as these books. Tina Allen-I met you in May 1996 in Clarke's Beach, Newfoundland, you are a true friend of mine. You may not see it now but I was there when you wanted to talk, we had the conversations together when we both went walking in the woods and talked about personal matters. The issues I will take to my grave and the same with you. I have wrong you in April 21, 2000 but I just want you to understand I am not perfect and still care about you. I miss you and I hope you are doing very well. Second, Victor Stevens-I first met you at Bingo in a small town in North River, Newfoundland in July, 2010. I have to say I enjoyed our times together, even though you were seventy-nine years old and you passed away in May of 2013, you were eighty-two. I was born on July 4, 1980 and you were born on July 7, 1930, fifty years in the difference, age means nothing to me as long that friendship is there, that is a memory for me to last the "ages".

I would like to mention to the lost souls in this world who have yet to discover their true finding and meaning for living. Your gift will come to you-have faith and believe like me. I used to be a lost soul myself at one point. Also I would like to thank Kwik-Kopy for working on all my books as well. I thank each staff member for their hard work and hours you all put in-thanks.

Lastly, I would like to thank my readers for reading my books. If you support me I will continue to support you as long my mind keeps thinking.

**ANDREW J. WILDING**
A.K.A. SCARECROW

# FOUR SOULS OF NATURE

## THE SEALED KINGDOM

# INTRO

Princess Annie-with nineteen years in as "Princess" and "Guardian" of all creatures, grew very sad outside but full of anger build up inside. She would often say to herself is why would the creatures make her a "Princess"? Are sayings that different or important to creatures of all kinds? She has everything that any human being has-food, clothes, shelter, company to talk to (if she wants it), privileges to history books at the keep where the Mermen live, respect, honor, trust-EVERYTHING.

But it all changes on one faithful night when Princess Annie is about to make her own "history". This last part of the whole series from the beginning of Scarecrow up until now, everything will make sense at the end of the day. It is broken into three different parts.

Princess Annie will be the true heroine and earn more then the title "Princess". She will be remembered for all time as the greatest figure in history-statutes of her image, books about what she is about to do and the important part is bring balance forever for everyone-both living and the dead (souls that is).

# CHAPTER 1

# SPIRIT FROM AN UNTOLD PAST

It was a very cold windy evening on this particular day. The sky was dark mixed with red (a sign it is going to be nice the next day). This day of the week lay on a Thursday, at 9:45 P.M. in the evening. Princess Annie gave herself so work to do because on this day she was just bored, the creatures did all the work around her "small" keep (her cottage/tree house is very large but small compare to other castles in the country of Hydra).

Princess Annie did some raking in the afternoon(leaves) and made some muffins while drinking one of her three favorite drinks-milk. She normally drinks milk in the afternoon, black tea in the evening and red wine before she goes to bed.

While sipping on her black tea, looking out her window in her quarters, she felt someone was watching her-it was one of the creatures. "Sorry to bother you Princess Annie but I was wondering if you need anything"? "No, but the next time my bedroom door is wide open, knock, I dislike being watched behind my back, understood" said Princess Annie, "Sorry, I will never happen again Princess Annie, happy a good night to you", said the creature. "And you as well. Close the door when you leave my quarters, good-bye", said Princess Annie, as she started to take another sip of her very strong black tea.

Princess Annie walked over to her mirror, sat down and started to comb her hair. Just when she finished her tea, she felt someone was watching her-AGAIN. "I told you to knock next time, how hard is that to understand and remember". There was no answer or response back to Princess Annie. "Did you not hear me"? said Princess Annie, getting angry for the moment.

"Yes I heard you the first time Princess Annie", said the voice. "And why didn't you answer me the first time"? said Princess Annie. "To be honest, I really didn't feel like answering you-sorry", said the voice. "WHAT! How dare you to speak to your Princess of the creatures", said Princess Annie, as she stood up by her mirror which was in the corner of her bed. When Princess Annie turn around, she didn't see a creature, she saw a spirit, just a cloud-like-mist, that is all.

"Who are you"? said Princess Annie, scared and confused at the same time. "Do not fear me child. I know who you are but you do not know who I am-not yet anyway, said the spirit. I also have a name but I am not going to tell you-yet. I have a request to ask you Princess Annie". "And what is that"? said Princess Annie, not so scared for the moment. "I want you to go to the Sealed Kingdom, don't worry I will give you the information before I leave here to where it is located. You don't have to do this but if you decided to go, it will all make sense when you arrive there-fare"? said the spirit.

Princess Annie stared at the spirit for a while and said, "Fine, I will go. I am bored silly staying here with nothing to do". "So true, said the spirit. But before I give you the information, you will encounter three strangers on your journey to the Sealed Kingdom-they will help you, maybe not right away at first but they will help you. Here are the three strangers profiles, maybe this will help you understand who you will encounter on your journey to the Sealed Kingdom-in order.

# PROFILES

**BEARD**
RACE: Plant. HEIGHT: 3 foot 10.
FACIAL FEATURES: Tree-like looks. WEIGHT: 95 lbs.
WEAPON AT HAND: Bow-n-arrow. EYES: Blue.
PERSONALITY: Very dry. HAIR: Long and yellow.
GENDER: Male.
COMBAT SKILLS: Very fast but not very strong.

**CHAINZ**
RACE: Creature-Troll.
FACIAL FEATURES: Very scarred, mammoth build.
HEIGHT: 6 foot 10. WEAPON AT HAND: Chains.
WEIGHT: 330 lbs.
PERSONALITY: Abrupt.
EYES: White. GENDER: Male.
HAIR: Red( only on the sides and bald on top). COMBAT
SKILLS: Very strong but slow.

**MALT**
RACE: Half human/ half doll.
FACIAL FEATURES; Looks like a doll. HEIGHT: 5 foot 5.
WEAPON AT HAND: None. WEIGHT: 155 lbs.
PERSONALITY: Soft spoken. EYES: Grey.
GENDER: Female. HAIR: Green
COMBAT SKILLS: None.

"I was going to ask you about this Sealed Kingdom but why spoil the fun, I love surprises just like now, don't you agree"? said Princess Annie. The spirit did not comment or say a word. "Here is a map to where the Sealed Kingdom is located, good luck child and remember you are not alone in this world and I will see and talk to you again, Princess Annie", said the spirit.

With that the spirit flashed a light in front of Princess Annie and then disappeared. "That was fun! The Sealed Kingdom? Maybe it is a kingdom for me? Who knows but I really need a holiday plus I know the location of the Sealed Kingdom but I have to see it to believe. The Lost Woods? Interesting! That spirit did not say what part of the past he or she is from-very interesting indeed", said Princess Annie.

Just when she was about to pour some red wine into her glass( she keeps all of her wine in her quarters), a voice came from nowhere and said to Princess Annie, "I forgot to mention to you, I will be your guide and I am a spirit of a past, a past that there is no record of, does that answer your question? Have a drink for me and I will see you at the Sealed Kingdom", the spirit.

Princess Annie raised her eyebrows and said to herself, "I guess it does answer my question.

Now that is very interesting, indeed". She poured her red wine into a glass and got another glass and pour some red wine in the second one and said, "Something tells me that this journey is going to be quite something and I hope it is good and not evil either".

## CHAPTER 2

# THE JOURNEY BEGINS

By the next morning, around 7:15 A.M., Princess Annie woke up, go out of bed, washed up, got dressed and headed to the living room area.

One of the servants of Princess Annie saw her and said, "Is everything all right, Princess Annie? It looks like your is spinning like wheels"?

Princess Annie looked back at the creature and answered, with a glare, "Maybe my mind is spinning like wheels". Princess Annie stood up from her chair by the fireplace and said to the creature, "I have to go away for awhile, it looks like I will be gone for more than a month and I am not saying where, it is private. Don't worry about me, I can handle myself into the wild. After all, my long sword will be with me, I hate to see my blade into someone else's belly if they want to be cute and all....ha".

The creature just stared at Princess Annie. "I have a request, yourself and the other creatures talk among yourselves who will be steward or stewardess of my keep in place of my absent, understand" said Princess Annie.

The creature answered back, "Yes, Princess Annie". "Good", said Princess Annie. And with that all said, Princess Annie got her belongings along with her long sword, threw a hooded cloak on her to hide her identity and off she went into the wild on the journey to the Sealed Kingdom.

# CHAPTER 3

---

# EVERY PATH HAS A ROOT

It was around 8:45 A.M. in the morning, Princess Annie left her keep around 7:45 A.M., an hour walking in the open plains on this cool breezy day.

There are going to be many different paths in this journey, a little too many, Princess Annie knows this a little too well (in the mind). Like gardener, for example, you plant a tree but it is not just planting it, it is the whole process from start to finish. You get a shovel, dig a hole, clean it out of all the roots and rocks, mixed with a chemical called Bone Meal (created by the Mermen, this helps the roots of any plant grow strong), you put a quarter of fresh soil in it, put the tree in the middle of the hole, add more fresh soil to the hole till you are at the top and finally add water to the plant.

Princess Annie is very scared inside but outside is calm as a flower. She only did this deed for the spirit because she thought the creatures, Mermen and everyone else (humans) would be in danger.

From start to finish, every root has a beginning but how long is the root? Will this root be short or long? Or will there be many roots to walk on. Only time will tell for this sad, unhappy soul.

# CHAPTER 4

---

# FIRST ENCOUNTER-BEARD

Princess Annie had to be walking for a good hour and a half till she came to a forest which is part of Lost Woods, on the outskirts or on the edge of the boundaries of this wooden realm.

Not tired at all, Princess Annie walked for about twenty minutes and suddenly she stop walking, dead in her traps. "I know someone or something is falling me. I am not stupid or should I say imagining it, I can sense it and you are scared as much as these old trees are, so come out, NOW", said Princess Annie, not letting her guard down.

Moments later a noise came out of the trees, Princess Annie turned around slowing, glaring as she did this. In front of her stood, not a human, not a creature but a walking, breathing tree. Princess Annie never saw this type of species before.

The tree was the same height as Princess Annie and before this tree had a chance to speak, Princess Annie said,

"You must be Beard, I have been expecting you. So tell me, what role to you have in this joyful journey, Beard"?

Beard walked up to Princess Annie and said, "I was going to ask you the same thing, Princess Annie". Princess Annie looked at him with her eyebrows raised. "I had an unexpected guest a few nights ago and said you will be here, told me everything about you", said Beard. "The same here by mine was last night", said Princess Annie, with a small grin on her face.

# CHAPTER 5

# BEARD-LAST OF HIS KIND

"I never knew there was a species of your kind living, I should be blessed or should I say why me and why now", said Princess Annie. Beard looked at Princess Annie while walking and said to her, "You should be blessed in that sense because you are the only one knows of my kind exists, I am the last of my kind to be living here on this planet".

Princess Annie looked back quick at Beard and said, "I didn't know......". "That's all right Annabelle. There are reasons why my kind is extinct. Pardon me if you don't mind if I call you Annabelle, I find it safer that way. I don't want anyone know you are a princess, it could danger us all", said Beard. "Not at all", said Princess Annie.

"As I was saying my kind in the past wasn't the blessed kind, we weren't evil, we just didn't agree with certain things in the past like us kind being guards to protect others wealth or homes or keeps. To us, in our own minds, we should have the freedom to do as we please, not be used as tools.

Back then, we were guardians of this planet but the other different species rise up against us and wiped us out except one-ME. The others protected me by cutting my root line so I won't be a giant like the others, before the war with the other species but we had friends too in the past in that war who tried to aid us and now they are gone as well. How I miss them so much. I just hope this Sealed Kingdom show some light or something or anything", said Beard.

"Likewise", said Princess Annie, as they pressed on deeper into the woods of the wild.

# CHAPTER 6

# SECOND ENCOUNTER-CHAINZ

"I have to say when my kind destroyed yours, you made fantastic firewood to get the heat going. Great heat to make weapons, I know, because I have been using them for centuries....ha", said a strange voice close by.

"WHO SAID THAT", shouted Beard. "Show yourself, only a coward hides and not faces a challenge into hiding", said Princess Annie. A few minutes later, jumping out of one of the trees, stood in front of them a huge mammoth build-like creature.

"You must be Chainz, yes"? said Princess Annie. "And you must be Princess Annie and Beard. My guess is that you all meet the same spirit just as I have and WE are in search of this Sealed Kingdom? It has taken myself two months to get here from the mountains and I thought I was dreaming at first, guess I was wrong", said Chainz.

"I was thinking of the same thing", said Beard. "I thought you were all killed off, my bad", said Chainz. "Sorry to disappoint you", said Beard.

Chainz answered back, "I really like surprises", getting mad for the moment. Princess Annie got in between both Beard and Chainz and said, "Do you both know each other"?

Both Beard and Chainz looked at Princess Annie. Beard spoken first, "I don't know Chainz and he doesn't know me but my kind fought against his kind many, many years ago". "And it wasn't just your kind either we fought. My breed fought many different kinds of species-I guess some for good and some for bad", said Chainz.

# CHAPTER 7

# CHAINZ-LAST OF HIS KIND

"You said you fought different kinds of species years ago, do you know how many"? said Princess Annie. "How am I supposed to know how many, I lost track. But I can tell you both one thing, in all my battles and fights I have been in, to me, Beards kind should have been left alone", said Chainz, while all three of them walk deeper into Lost Woods.

"And why didn't your kind leave us alone then"? said Beard. Chainz paused for a moment and later said, "We all felt threaten because of your kinds height and strength, that is all. Later I learned your kind is peaceful folk from the others but something's are a little too late if you ask me". "You can said that again", said Princess Annie, raising her eyebrows. "You shouldn't use your royal name, it is dangerous right out into the wild", said Chainz. "Annabelle will do", said Princess Annie, looking over her shoulder at Beard.

"I guess myself and Beard here have something in common", said Chainz. "And what is that"? said Beard. "You and I are the last of our own kind", said Chainz. "That is very interesting", said Princes Annie. "Beard and Chainz are the last survivors each of their own kind. My guess is that our third guest we be the FIRST or LAST of their kind".

Beard and Chainz looked over at Princess Annie of what she has said. "How did you become the last of your kind"? said Beard. Chainz looked at Beard and said, "A mixed of old age, greed and power, end of story. I would rather not get into it, lets us just keep walking. I hope this Sealed Kingdom will give myself an answer or two in why I am here with you two in this gloomy part of the world".

# CHAPTER 8

---

# THIRD ENCOUNTER-MALT

With an half an hour in of walking, all three of them came very close the village of Cherry Blossom, which no creature lives here now because of the events of the past with King Scarecrow (the fake one). It is just a memorial place in respect of the greeting with the real Scarecrow or should I say in respect to him.

"So you three are going to the Sealed Kingdom as well"? said a voice close by. "Who said that, who is there, show yourself or is it Malt I am talking to"? said Princess Annie. "You are correct Princess Annie and the other two are Beard and Chainz, yes"? said Malt.

A few minutes later, out of the woods, came out which look like a doll but at the same time a human but much more less a doll figure stood in front of all three of them. "So the spirit is right but I would never guess there would be a living, breathing doll-like-human", said Princess

Annie. Beard and Chainz nodded their heads up and down, agreeing with what Princess Annie has just said.

"It is very nice to meet all of you here. I just arrive here about five minutes ago, I live very close by, actually I live right in the heart of Cherry Blossom", said Malt. "This area is off-limits", said Princess Annie. "I know but I live in that big white tree and no I did not cut a hole out of it to make it a home, I came "from" that cherry blossom tree", said Malt, as all three looked at each other puzzled.

# CHAPTER 9

## MALT-FIRST OF HER KIND

"What do you mean you came out of that cherry blossom tree, I have been living here in this part of the woods for centuries and you are the first time I have seen you", said Beard. "I am new here so I have no idea what is really going on here", said Chainz. "Actually I am the first of my kind", said Malt. Princess Annie looked over at Beard and Malt, with her eyebrows raised and later said, "Very interesting of you to say that. We have Beard and Chainz here, the last of their kind, Malt here the first of her kind and myself, a first-time commoner with no royal blood in me, crowns "Princess" of all the creatures. Two "FIRSTS" and two "LASTS", interesting indeed".

While walking, getting very close to the memorial site of the village of Cherry Blossom, Malt started to talk a little about herself. "I was cursed for a very long time. You see I discovered the Sealed Kingdom by chance when I was very young. For doing so I was cursed to look like a doll, a doll I used to play with when I was a child. When I was cursed I lost all memory of the Sealed Kingdom, the only thing I remember is just the reason why I was cursed. I also remember is that I was stuck in this particular tree until the time has come for the tree to release me and here I am. I remember Scarecrow coming to the village of Cherry Blossom and the creatures of the past as well".

All three, Princess Annie, Beard and Chainz did not comment or say a word of what Malt have said.

# CHAPTER 10

---

# UNDERGROUND PASSAGE TO THE SEALED KINGDOM

"So where is this Sealed Kingdom"? said Chainz. "The spirit gave us all information that it would be somewhere here but where"? said Beard. For a moment, Princess Annie examined the cherry blossom tree, walked around it a few times but did not say a word. "What are you doing Princess Annie"? said Malt. "Call me Annabelle please, any royal name could be dangerous out in the wild", said Princess Annie. "Sorry Annabelle", said Malt.

"This is just an educational guess but maybe this Sealed Kingdom is underneath this cherry blossom tree, after all, it is "different" compare to the rest of the trees and only "one" of their kind", said Princess Annie. After a minute or two every flower fell from the cherry blossom tree, landed on the ground, went into the ground and formed a passageway under the ground.

"You are right, Annabelle", said Beard. "Good job", said Malt. "Never judge someone by their size, they are full of surprises...ha", said Chainz, as all four walked down the staircase under the cherry blossom tree.

When all four got to the bottom of the stair-case made out of tree root, they came to a huge giant plaque and a few distance away was a huge giant door with a creature engraved in it. All four never saw a creature like this before. It look like half squid and half creature. Before Princess Annie, Beard, Chainz and Malt entered through the door, they read the plaque called "History of the Sealed Kingdom" and here is what is reads.

# CHAPTER 11

# HISTORY OF THE SEALED KINGDOM

" In the beginning there was nothing, just rock and soil everywhere. I came from a distance galaxy where no man or living thing knows about.

When I arrived here, it was just me. In respect to this planet made of rock and soil, I decided to make myself a kingdom underground for no one to know about and so it was called "The Sealed Kingdom". In time, when the time is right, it will be known to man and living species everywhere but only those worthy will find it. It will be the four souls of this planet, four elements-EARTH, FIRE, WIND and WATER-this is what the planet is made out of. It could be one soul with all four of these elements OR one for each soul-time will tell".

"Behind this giant door is a world I have collected over the years, some from this planet and some from species I have created. When you enter the door you will walk out of here "change"-both physically and mentally. The four elements of nature will do this to you one way or the other, but for good and not for evil".

"What you will see are reminders of nature and species alike. When you reach your goal here in the Sealed Kingdom, you know what the goal will be. The kingdom is sealed for a reason because there are some things I do not want extinct or destroyed, so I "sealed" them in my "kingdom"=Sealed Kingdom, good catch I think".

"I would like to mention is that it was I who created all the different species here on this planet. There are twenty-nine all together but a lot of them did not get along with each other so they killed off, one-by-one, specie-after-specie until their was only a handful left. Only three kinds remain alive-humans, creatures and Mermen".

"I never wanted any of this to happen-bloodshed, greed, power, fighting. All I wanted was peace and harmony, nothing more and nothing less".

"The souls from the great battle of the twenty-nine are collected here in the Sealed Kingdom. So one day who will be the ruler of this planet-one of the four souls of the elements OR the ONE soul-can bring these souls to life again to live here on the planet again".

"In the past there was a great battle from the twenty-nine species, what a battle it was indeed. When you travel through the grounds of the Sealed Kingdom and inside as well, I will personally show you OR all four of you the full battle and all the information of the twenty-nine species who fought in it as well".

"I have seen and witnessed too much in my lifetime and if I could erase all the evil, I would in a heartbeat".

"Lastly, I would like to mention it was I who gave this planet a name, it is called Kraken. I named it after me for my divine powers, size, speed and more importantly my image".

"I just hope that yourself OR four of you can understand my position I am in. To me, I am not worthy of such power but you are-so I decided to divide my powers into four elements to represent this planet Kraken. If it all goes to one soul, he or she will be the new king or queen but if each element finds four souls then it could be a bit complicated. You OR all four of you will understand when you reach the end of your journey here both in and out of the Sealed Kingdom. Personally, I hope it is one soul and not four different souls, you will understand like I said before".

"If you are the chosen one OR chosen ones, you have a special gift, a gift you probably not yet discovered. If it is four souls it will be two FIRSTS of that kind and two LASTS of that kind. Two LASTS means one from species and only ones alive from that species. Two FIRSTS means two of these species are the first in history on this planet to become someone or something which no one dare dream possible which would never happen".

"And again you will understand EVERYTHING at the end of your journey. Thank-you for reading and best of luck".

*King Kraken-Founder and Guardian of the planet Kraken*

# CHAPTER 12

---

# WEATHER

All four of them paused for a moment, looking at each other. "We better get moving than", said Princess Annie, as Beard, Chainz and Malt nodded their heads up and down as all four of them open this huge giant door.

Once inside, all four could not believe what they were experiencing. Thunder, lightning, rain and some-what windy-underground. All four are nervous and scared, doesn't matter how tough you are. They were all thinking of the same thing-this is not normal to have weather like this underground.

The weather here would not take a break.

Every second-"CRASH", "BANG", "BOOM"-not normal at all. The rain felt very cold but the wind was very cool not cold. The lightning was no ordinary lightning, it look red not yellow.

Up ahead all four saw a plaque with a description written on it, it reads.....

"The weather here is a sigh of anger, greed, power and violence. It was made by the twenty-nine species that lived here from the very beginning. Pray you don't end like this".

*King Kraken*

# CHAPTER 13

---

# TREES-OLD AND NEW

"My guess is that there are going to be more than one plaque along the way", said Princess Annie. Beard, Chainz and Malt agreed of what Princess Annie just said.

After a while of walking, the weather ease off until there was no more thunder, lightning, rain and some-what hard wind.

About tens minutes of walking, all four came to a wooded area. All they saw was different kinds of trees. Some look new, some look old and others mixed with old-n-new. And another plaque with a description written on it, it reads.....

"These trees are a sign of peace, sadness and hope. These species never wanted war but they are all killed off because of their facial features. Very sad and still trying to find peace and hope".

*King Kraken*

"Beard slowing turn around to look at Chainz, with a glare that could kill, even the dead itself.

"I know what you are thinking Beard and I agree with you one-hundred percent with your anger on me but my kind wasn't the only ones who attack at your kind. All I can say is that I am sorry about the past and I am not expecting any forgiveness from you", said Chainz. Beard did not comment or say a word to Chainz of what he said. "We should press on to see what is up ahead, ok"? said Malt.

# CHAPTER 14

---

# MUSHROOMS

All four continued to the Sealed Kingdom. When they all left the wooded area of trees, they all came to a field of mushrooms. These weren't ordinary mushrooms, they were all in different colors-red, blue, yellow, orange, brown, purple, pink, grey, black, white, bronze, silver and gold.

"What beauty"! said Princess Annie. "What a view"! said Beard. "Amazing sight"! said Malt. I must say, they may look like mushrooms but really they are a special breed, feels like....love", said Chainz.

Up ahead, all four saw another plaque in plain sight with a description written on it, it reads.....

"These mushrooms represent all of the different kinds of species that used to live here. Some are alive, while the rest of them are extinct but they should not be forgotten.

Mushrooms grow from the dead, like bodies, so I think this is a great fitting for them all".

*King Kraken*


Princess Annie, Beard, Chainz and Malt bow their heads down in respect of the fallen. After they all continued on their way to the Sealed Kingdom.

# CHAPTER 15

# OLD STONE

After they paid there respects, not far ahead is a huge piece of stone. When they all got there, on the stone were hand prints of all the different kinds of species that live on the planet of Kraken-twenty-six of them on one side and then another three more on the other side of the stone. The stone was no ordinary one, it look like it was made out of a rare mineral, mixed with Earth, Fire, Water and Wind because the stone would change colors. First it would be a dark brown stone, than a fire stone, than a water stone and than a white stone.

In front of this huge stone is a plaque with a description written on it, it reads.....

"This stone shows all the twenty-nine species who live and used to live here. I personally lay each hand print onto the stone, which I personally found right in the middle of this planet, mixed with Earth, Fire, Water and Wind. It shows who lived and still living here and remember for all eternity".

*King Kraken*


Princess Annie, Beard, Chainz and Malt bow their heads again in respect, not saying a word to each other and continued on their way.

# CHAPTER 16

---

# SWAMP OF SOULS

Just up ahead, in a distance all four saw what it look like a swamp. When they got there, the swamp did not stink or for that matter did not smell bad, not at all. The swamp was very damp, flowers in it but when they got even closer to the swamp, in the water they all saw different creatures of all kinds, like souls, resting in the waters in this particular swamp.

"What are they doing here"? said Malt, shaking her head left to right. "These is another plaque up ahead, lets read it and it will tells us all why they are here", said Beard.

So all four went up to the plaque, on the description here is what is written, it reads.....

"Here you will see souls of the fallen, in the greatest war this planet has witnessed, including myself. These souls are here because they can't find peace. I brought them here, hoping to rid their guilt of what they all have done in the past and when they find their peace, they will go to the afterlife with the others. Only they can admit their guilt, not myself ".

*King Kraken*


"They are not the only ones feeling guilty of what they have done", said Chainz. No one did not say a word and continued on their way.

# CHAPTER 17

# INSIDE THE SEALED KINGDOM

About fifteen minutes when all four left the swamp full of souls, in a short distance they all saw a huge silver looking castle. "This must be the Sealed Kingdom...nice", said Princess Annie. "What craft work in such a castle", said Chainz, with one knee on the ground. "It is defiantly a symbol of power", said Beard. "I just hope the inside of the Sealed Kingdom is kind to us all", said Malt.

All four went up to the doors of the Sealed Kingdom, made out of silver. Before one of them was about to knock on the doors, it opened by itself. All four looked at each other nervously and then started to enter the Sealed Kingdom.

Inside the Sealed Kingdom, there were crystal chandeliers everywhere, the floor made out of marble and everything else is made out of silver mixed with gold. It was huge, a castle for a King of Kings or Queen of Queens. It is a castle like no other, makes the other castles and keeps on this planet look like toothpicks(figure of speech).

This castle has many layers in it, like levels. A spiral staircase led to each level. It looked like, in a distance, a plaque on each level but, to them, they didn't see ANYTHING on each level so why have a plaque there?

"More plaques? How many are there"? said Chainz. "What is the rush", said Beard. King Kraken is just telling us all about the Sealed Kingdom", said Malt. "Or maybe King Kraken is more than meets the eye", said Princess Annie, leading the way to the first level of the castle.

# CHAPTER 18

---

# FOUNTAIN OF SPECIES

On the first level of the Sealed Kingdom, there was a very large fountain, formed in different shapes and in different sizes, not only that but in different colors as well. Whichever the water flow through in the different size and shape of that symbol, it would change color. There was also another plaque, just like the others outside the Sealed Kingdom, a description is written on it, it reads.....

"This fountain represents the twenty-nine species. Each color and symbol gives meaning to each specie. Some are happiness, power, leadership and yes, some are even control, greed and fame. But not one of them is a symbol of violence, and bloodshed. I just hope this fountain can bring peace to every specie but I can only hope, that is all".

*King Kraken*

"I wonder what symbol and color I am"? said Malt. "Hard to tell", said Beard. "I didn't know we had a color and a symbol that represents each species", said Chainz. "That's nice, lets move on to the second level, shall we"? said Princess Annie, leading the way.....again.

Malt just rolled her eyes, Beard shaking his head left to right and Chainz just followed and said to himself, "She has more anger build inside then I do".

# CHAPTER 19

---

# MUSIC OF ALL KINDS

On the second level of the Sealed Kingdom, there were pianos-EVERYWHERE. One each piano were a symbol and color, representing a specie. There were twenty-nine pianos altogether. Some were small and some were big but all of them were made out of silver. A plaque was there with a description written on it, it reads.....

"Twenty-nine pianos with twenty-nine different tones of music. Some are happy, sad, and alone. In respect to them all, I have no favorite one to pick from but there is one thing I can say about these twenty-nine different tones of music towards nature-they have a reason to live which is important to me and also to them".

*King Kraken*

"What beauty"! said Malt. "What craft work in all of these pianos", said Chainz. "Off to the next level, shall we"? said Princess Annie. "Show some heart and respect Annabelle", said Beard.

Princess Annie turned around to look at all three of her traveling companions and said, "Not showing heart and respect doesn't mean I have it, don't you agree"? Beard, Chainz and Malt did not comment or say a word back at Princess Annie.

Off they went to the third level of the Sealed Kingdom.

# CHAPTER 20

---

# RARE PICTURES OF SPECIES

On the third level of the Sealed Kingdom, right in plain view in of Princess Annie, Beard, Chainz and Malt, all around them were pictures of each species, twenty-nine of them. All four could not believe what they are seeing. Species they have never seen before (except their own kind).

"I have lived a long life but I never saw as many in my life", said Chainz. "Same here", said Beard. "I was stuck in that cherry blossom tree so this is the first time for me", said Malt. "All I can say about these pictures is that they are not forgotten and oh.....here is another plaque, surprise, surprise", said Princes Annie, walking towards the plaque along with Beard, Chainz and Malt. The description written on it reads.....

"Here I have a picture of all the species who live here, one from each species to be exact. I wanted this done here in the Sealed Kingdom because to show my love for each one of them and to be remember for all time".

*King Kraken*


"My kind is here", said Beard. "And my kind is here", said Chainz. "I think I am here but I am not too sure about it", said Malt. "You are probably right you are the first of your kind, in a way. You are half human and half creature, who knows"? said Princess Annie, walking to the next level of the Sealed Kingdom. "True", said Malt talking to herself.

# CHAPTER 21

---

# BUILDERS OF THE SEALED KINGDOM

On the fourth level of the Sealed Kingdom, there were names all over the walls, too many to count. Names that Princess Annie and Malt can't pick out but Beard and Chainz pick out same of the names on the walls (in their own language).

Again there was a plaque there with a description written on it, it reads.....

"Here are the names of the different species that help build this fine castle, the Sealed Kingdom. There are about five thousand names written on these walls, five thousand hard-working men and women, gave their passion, honor and even work as a team. I myself gave the finishing touches on it. I covered the castle inside-out with silver and yes everyone help me as well. Thank-you all for your hard work you will be remember for all eternity".

*King Kraken*

"If this is not respect then what is it", said Beard. "Five thousand workers....WOW", said Malt. "I am speechless", said Chainz, shaking his head left to right. "It is nice for King Kraken to show his respect to his creations. Come, we all have a ways to go before we all get to the top of this keep", said Princess Annie.

# CHAPTER 22

---

# GIANT PUMPKIN

On the fifth level of the Sealed Kingdom, there is a giant pumpkin but not just a ordinary pumpkin but in different colors. Some pumpkins are orange, green and white these days. This pumpkin even glowed in colors as well. A plaque was there with a description written on it, it reads.....

"This giant pumpkin houses all the species into one. To me, they are my children under the same roof. I hope that they all stay together as one so I have a color from each species and added to this giant pumpkin. I think it really stands out but I guess some things in life you shouldn't mixed".

King Kraken

"You are so right about that, King Kraken", said Princess Annie, as she started to go through her belongings and taken out a small fan, waving it in her face. Beard, Chainz and Malt did not comment or say a word. "Shall we move on to the next level"? said Princess Annie, while walking toward another set of a spiral staircase.

# CHAPTER 23

---

# DOLLS

On the sixth level of the Sealed Kingdom, there were dolls, twenty-nine of them. Very big in size. Looking exactly like that particular specie-creature, human, troll, tree, etc. A plaque was there with a description written on it, it reads.....

"I have made twenty-nine dolls to represent each specie. These dolls look like that of the species and I made them because deep down in our hearts and soul we are children all over-young and old. I believe all of us are children and why do I believe this because I have yet to discover that I am still a child. I always take things seriously. If I just sit down and think, maybe one day at one point in my life, I too was a child".

*King Kraken*

"I wonder if I was at this level of the Sealed Kingdom, playing with these dolls. Maybe that is why I am cursed by looking like a doll", said Malt. "Probably", said Beard. "Makes sense if you ask me", said Chainz. "That's what most children do, play with dolls, girls mostly not boys. Anyway we all should be moving on, we still have a ways to go", said Princess Annie.

# CHAPTER 24

# SNOWFLAKES

On the seventh level of the Sealed Kingdom, Princess Annie, Beard, Chainz and Malt could not believe what they saw with their own eyes-SNOWFLAKES-falling down from the ceiling on this particular level of the Sealed Kingdom. But these were no ordinary snowflakes, they were all in different colors, some a full color and some were mixed. A plaque was there with a description written on it, it reads.....

"When I traveled through of what I have created, the most beautiful thing I have seen with my own eyes are snowflakes. They are so gentle, so peaceful and so full of memory. They come in different sizes and shapes. They spend days, months and years in the skies, collecting experience and knowledge. That is when I started to think of the twenty-nine species I have created, they are all of that too".

*King Kraken*

"King Kraken really loves of what he has created", said Malt, with a tear roll down her face. "True", said Beard. "I wonder if he is still alive"? said Chainz. "Or maybe it could be the guilt he is suffering, who knows", said Princess Annie. Beard, Chainz and Malt nodded their heads up and down agreeing of what Princess Annie just said.

# CHAPTER 25

# CRYSTAL FIGURES

On the eighth level of the Sealed Kingdom, there were figures of different kinds of species, twenty-nine of them made out of crystal. The work that was put in making these figures was something else. Up, down, left, right and center-PERFECT. There was a plaque there with a description written on it, it reads.....

"I have made crystal figures of each species I have created, twenty-nine of them. To me, they are crystals into perfection. A crystal-very firm, very particular, like the water very still-looks like a mirror at times. You can see right through it, just like the species I have created, I can see right through them. What they are thinking and kind of soul they have as well"

*King Kraken*

"I don't know about you guys but I find this pretty creepy", said Chainz. "In a way but at the same time it could represent a gift they have and yet to discover in life", said Beard. "Or maybe it is a sign like they are hurting from the inside", said Malt. "Or maybe it is a sign that we should move on to the next level and see what is up there", said Princess Annie. Beard and Chainz just glared at Princess Annie while she walked away and Malt just rolled her eyes and shock her head left to right.

# CHAPTER 26

# WEAPONS

On the ninth level of the Sealed Kingdom, there were weapons-EVERYWHERE. The weapons were placed by each symbol to represent each specie. Some have a lot of weapons and some had only one weapon. Each species were good or great with these weapons of their origin. A plaque was there with a description written on it, it reads.....

"I have personally placed these weapons of each of the species of which they were able to use in combat. Also it is a reminder, to me, how awful it is to make these weapons, to take a life away with these weapons. How cruel but at the same time these weapons make peace but I wish it didn't have to come to this point, in my mind, to make such horrible tools against nature itself. Who would think of this? Was it I who thought of these weapons? After all I did created all the species here on this planet, so maybe I DID created these tools".

*King Kraken*

"While others find weapons relaxing. Look at Jeremy Andrews A.K.A. Scarecrow, he made them on his spare time, according to the history books at the Mermen keep", said Princess Annie. Beard, Chainz and Malt did not comment or say a word.

# CHAPTER 27

---

# BLACK WATER

On the tenth level of the Sealed Kingdom, there was a huge pool of water but the water is different, it is black as oil. It is defiantly water and not oil because the way it was shifting back and forth. A plaque was there with a description written on it, it reads.....

"I put a pool here, filled it with water but I change the water to black because of the sadness and sins of the twenty-nine species I have created. Not only their sins and sadness but mine as well. I am not perfect myself in a lot of ways, I think I have wronged them all and it is my fault, not them. So I blame myself and only me, no one else".

*King Kraken*

"And I thought it was me that water is black as oil, funny. Poor King Kraken, feel sorry for the powerful and not the weak.....yeah......right......sure", said Princess Annie, as she headed to the next level. Beard, Chainz and Malt just looked over at each other and finally Malt said to both Beard and Chainz, in a low voice. "That child is hurting". "She is not the only one who is hurting", said Chainz, as he left to go to the next level. Beard looked over at Malt and said, "We are all hurting, it is how you deal with it in life". "True"! said Malt.

# CHAPTER 28

---

# CREATURE

On the eleventh level of the Sealed Kingdom, there was a picture and a statue of a creature. It is not a creature that Princess Annie, Beard, Chainz and Malt. Saw before. It is not even one of the twenty-nine species either. This creature looked like a dragon but no arms and legs and the ears looks like fins from a fish or something. A plaque was with a description written on it, it reads.....

"This creature or species is my pet called Hydra. It is the guardian of this planet. This beast has power like no other. Breathes dark blue fire, can move faster than light and the scales on the Hydra's body are as thick as blood mixed with silver. The species of this creature is also called Hydra, which means "Water King". There is only one of his kind. I will tell you more about this Hydra. I guess, in a sense I have discovered him. It will make sense at the end of the day. When you progress higher in the Sealed Kingdom, you will understand".

*King Kraken*


"Maybe that is why they named this country and castle, Hydra. Maybe the Mermen knew something about this beast, who knows. And King Kraken NEVER created this Hydra either, very interesting, I must say", said Princess Annie. "What a beast indeed", said Chainz. "I wonder if it is still alive"? said Malt. "Hydra means "Water King". I wonder if the Mermen ever met this Hydra. After all, both creatures live underwater and I assume "Water King" means underwater", said Beard. Princess Annie, Chainz and Malt nodded their heads up and down agreeing of what Beard has just said.

# CHAPTER 29

---

# THE CROWN OF KRAKEN

On the twelfth level of the Sealed Kingdom, there was a good-size crown sitting on a platter, made mostly out of silver with a small mixed with gold. There were also diamonds, emeralds and rubies on it as well. A plaque was there with a description written on it, it reads....

"This crown here represents the twenty-nine species that I have created in honor of them. The colors on the crown show for each specie, some are whole, others are mixed. I used to wear this crown regularly but since that great war of the twenty-nine species, I lost interest. Th only time I will wear this crown is that when all twenty-nine species reunite all as one but that will never happen. All I can do is pray and hope for the better, that is all".

*King Kraken*

"What a crown! I never saw any crown like this before", said Beard. "Me either", said Chainz. "It looks heavy but yet it looks light", said Malt. "A crown is a crown, a status symbol, a symbol of power, that is all. I am not being rude or being disrespectful but it is only the truth. Next level, shall we"? said Princess Annie. "What is her problem"? said Malt, talking very low to Beard and Chainz. "Maybe she did not get a crown"? said Beard, with his shoulders raised up. "Or maybe she hates being royalty? Who knows and who cares", said Chainz

# CHAPTER 30

---

# POWER OF SOULS

On the thirteenth level of the Sealed Kingdom, Princess Annie, Beard, Chainz and Malt could not believe what they were all seeing with their own eyes. They all saw what is appears to be a huge crystal ball with different colors in it. Inside the ball were hundreds, thousands, maybe millions of souls inside this huge crystal ball. A plaque was there with a description written on it, it reads.....

"This crystal ball here houses all the souls I have collected from the fallen over the years. I have learned that souls from living species have special gifts-three to be exact. One is to create a powerful weapon, second is to create a powerful life form and third is creator a new creator. Two have been completed. My pet Hydra I have created by the souls power. Second is the "Flame of Creation". I am just waiting for that "ONE" of the four elements from this planet-maybe one or four different ones-who knows".

*King Kraken*


"I can't believe this. King Kraken created the "Flame of Creation", nice to know. So Hope and the others didn't created it, it was King Kraken, he made out that they had created that sword. Come on, lets move to the next level", said Princess Annie, walking fast this time. Beard, Chainz and Malt just stared at Princess Annie for a moment and continued on their way to the next level.

# CHAPTER 31

# KEEPER OF THE SEALED KINGDOM

On the fourteenth level of the Sealed Kingdom, all four saw a huge picture, which appears to be King Kraken himself. He looked human, not a creature or for that matter any other kind of species at all. Everyone thought King Kraken was that creature on the huge doors, before they all enter the grounds of the Sealed Kingdom, the half squid/half creature engraved on it. A plaque was there with a description written on it, it reads.....

"This picture here is....me, King Kraken. I am human, not a creature of any kind. For the record, humans are not my favorite kind, I have no favorite kind, all equal to me. I am six feet tall, long white silver hair, blue eyes, I dress proper all the time and always in white and black, with long silver boots. Plus I am an expert with the "Katana" sword. A ancient sword that only a few can handle and I am one of that few. When the right time has come, I will meet that ONE or all four of the elements of nature".

*King Kraken*


"To me, King Kraken looks like Annabelle", said Beard. "I was thinking the same thing", said Chainz. "Maybe you are related to him, Annabelle", said Malt. Princess Annie walked up a little closer to the picture and said, "In a way he does but if he is related to me, than I am the next new Queen of that pet of his, that Hydra. I am not that sad looking, guilt eating, power hungry figure. His eyes say it all if you look carefully at them or for that matter, ANYONE'S eyes. Him and me the same, not one bit, thank-you very much", with her eyebrows raised.

Beard, Chainz and Malt just looked at Princess Annie. Later, all four went to the next level and would appear to be the final level of the Sealed Kingdom.

# CHAPTER 32

# THE ASH-COVERED TREE

On the fifteenth and final level of the Sealed Kingdom, Princess Annie, Beard, Chainz and Malt saw something which looked very familiar. There was a medium-size tree on the final level and it looked like that cherry blossom tree outside, on the surface of the entrance to get down here of the Sealed Kingdom. The same looks-big, blood red flowers that look like cherries and the tree as white as a ghost. A plaque was there with a description written on it, it reads.....

"Finally, the last stage of the Sealed Kingdom. This tree here is a symbol and image, just like the one outside. It is white because it is the ashes of the fallen from the great war between the species but that was centuries ago. The big red flowers are a reminder of the bloodshed and tears that was also in the great war. It almost looks like cherries if you ask me. Also there is a book in the next room through the doors, read it and it will show you or all four of you the great war that began before your time. So maybe, if you think about it, two levels into one but there is a reason for that, you or all four of you will understand".

*King Kraken*


"Lets just go through this door and read this book. Something tells me there is more to this cherry blossom than meets the eye", said Princess Annie, as all four opened the doors and entered the room on the same and final level.

# CHAPTER 33

---

# HISTORY ABOUT LOST WOODS

"This ash-covered tree here has a name and the name is Lost Woods. Lost Woods used to be a living, breathing, walking and a great leader of the tree like kind. He was often called "The Wise Tree" because of his knowledge and wisdom. He was never a white tree from the beginning, he became white all-over when he passed away in the great war against the other species. Lost Woods had a special gift and that gift is he can see things before that happen".

"You see Lost Woods saw the future of every species, including King Kraken himself. When Lost Woods came to King Kraken with this knowledge about the future, King Kraken grew nervous about this information. So King Kraken went to all the twenty-nine species personally and said to them all not to worry about the future because his is the creator and not Lost Woods".

"But before King Kraken went to the twenty-nine species about Lost Woods gift, Lost Woods mentioned to him that each specie will fight each other to the death for the sake of one-mans-greed of power and that one man is King Kraken said Lost Woods. So King Kraken formed his own army and so did Lost Woods but Lost Woods wanted peace and at the same time so did King Kraken. At the end of the day King Kraken thought he created a bad seed of evil and didn't want to accept the facts from Lost Woods".

"King Kraken didn't tell the full truth to his army because he thought everything he has created would end, like rock and soil when he got here to this planet. King Kraken convinced twenty-four species on his side and Lost Woods had the other five species on his side. Lost Woods was totally outnumbered but his army survived, three out of five-the Mermen, the creatures and the humans.

King Kraken was defeated, the founder and creator of the twenty-nine species, a creation defected a creator-go figure".

"Lastly there is a reason why Lost Woods is called this name. "LOST" means King Kraken has no knowledge or wisdom of any kind-just knows how the make things or in better terms no common sense how to control power and didn't accept help from a creation-he would feel embarrassed about it. "WOODS" means shelter the weak from the strong, like hiding in the shadows. Or also it could mean when the enemy can't see you and when the time is right-go to safety OR attack".

"If King Kraken seek help, none of this wouldn't happen at all-everyone would be alive here right now-that's too bad if you as me".

Written by: *Ork, Head Of The Mermen*

P.S. "I am so sorry for not listening to you, my friend Lost Woods. I will see you again and you will forever be missed".

*King Kraken*

Princess Annie, Beard, Chainz and Malt did not comment or say a word after reading this book about Lost Woods. All they did is shake their heads left to right and walk away.

# FOUR SOULS OF NATURE

## TWENTY-NINE ARMIES

# INTRO

This second part of this story takes place when Princess Annie, Beard, Chainz and Malt finished reading, "The History of Lost Woods", speechless and at the same time sick to their stomachs.

In the same room, all four discovered there are two crystal balls-very huge in size. ONE of the crystal balls will show all four the great war that happen centuries ago-it is called, "The Twenty-Nine Armies". What will Princess Annie, Beard, Chainz and Malt discover from the twenty-nine armies? Will they find something different that was not mention from the book they all read?

Only time will tell.

# CHAPTER 34

# TWO HUGE CRYSTAL BALLS

"WOW", said Chainz "I don't know what to say", said Beard. "What can we say"? said Malt. "I am not surprised at all. When we all started this little journey here, King Kraken, one-by-one, showing guilt. Just look at all these plaques we all have read, that said it all", said Princess Annie.

In a distance, all four discovered two huge crystal balls with a plaque for each one. "MORE plaques"? said Beard. "Plaques, plaques and more plaques", said Chainz. "Its getting too much if you ask me", said Malt.

Princess Annie went over first to the two huge crystal balls and said, "One is blank and the other says "Twenty-Nine Armies" written on the plaque". Beard, Chainz and Malt went over to the crystal ball with the description written on the plaque that said twenty-nine armies. A few seconds later, that crystal ball glowed in different colors.

The plaque change then suddenly a description appeared on it, it reads.....

"If you are the chosen ONE or chosen FOUR of the four elements-EARTH, FIRE, WATER and WIND-place your hand on this huge crystal ball and it will show you information on each species. The first five are from Lost Woods Army and the remaining twenty-four are from King Krakens Army".

"Time to get educated", said Princess Annie. "I am with you", said Beard. "Myself as well", said Chainz. "Don't forget me", said Malt.

So all four placed their hand on the crystal ball and suddenly a beam of light went into each individual head of the four hopefuls of nature.

Princess Annie, Beard, Chainz and Malt fell softly onto the floor. Here is the information all four received from the crystal ball. All twenty-nine species, twenty-nine armies, twenty-nine fighting mainly out of.....FEAR.

# CHAPTER 35

# FIRST FIVE ARMIES-LOST WOODS ARMY

## #1:TREE-ELK

Very tall and well-build. There specialty in combat is bow-n-arrows and clubs. There personality is very quiet and well-manner. They train often, just in case a fight is about to happen and very well-discipline too. Leaders Name: Lost Woods

## #2:THE MERMEN

Some are tall and some are average, very well-build. There specialty in combat is the trident, bow-n-arrows, and their shields. There personality is very quiet, very anti-social, they don't mix well with others. They train everyday, day and night, into perfection. Leaders Name: Ork.

# #3:CREATURES

They come in different sizes and some are physically strong and others are average. There specialty in combat is swords, bow-n-arrows, shields, maces, clubs and axes. There personality is very friendly, out-going and easy to mix with. They train in different ways-some of them go to the limit while others train sometimes(if they had to go further in training ,in hours, they would). Leaders Name: They have no leader, they all work as one.

# #4:HUMANS

Almost the same as the creatures, except their facial features. They come in different sizes, some are physically strong and others are average .There specialty in combat is swords, bow-n-arrows, shields, maces, clubs and axes. There personality is very friendly, out-going and easy to mix with. They train sometimes in groups and by themselves sometimes. Leaders Name: Alexander Von Hearst.

# #5:INSECTAS

They come in different sizes, some as big as the Mermen, others as big as a thumb nail. There specialty in combat is swords and bow-n-arrows. There personality can be friendly and sometimes they can be very stubborn. They train everyday, sometimes when they are working, they would practice with the creatures. Leaders Name: Ant-Lion.

This concludes the information on Lost Woods Army. The next are King Krakens Army, twenty-four species. A lot of them are non-trained or just started to train. Almost a last minute notice (- figure of speech).

# CHAPTER 36

---

# FIRST TEN ARMIES OF KING KRAKEN

## #1:TROLLS

Very tall and heavy build. There specialty in combat is chains they are the only type of species to use them. There personality is abrupt and can be rude at times. They train off-n-on but they are not determine like other species. Leaders Name: Moth.

## #2:GOBLINS

Medium size height and weight. There specialty in combat is clubs. They personality is a lot of times very sour, an odd-time something positive out of their mouth. They train sometimes by themselves and sometimes with the Trolls. Leaders Name: Brew.

# #3:LIGHTERS

Very small, like a ball. There specialty in combat is bright light, they can blind others for a brief moment in time. There personality is very quiet. They do no training at all. Leaders Name: Brite.

# #4:DARKERS

Same as the Lighters. Very small in size. There specialty in combat is dark light, they can blind others for a brief moment in time. There personality is very quiet. They do no training at all. Leaders Name: Nite.

# #5:CLAWERS

They are feline type. They are average height but physically in shape. There speciality in combat is their claws and knives. There personality is very well-manner. They have little training. Leaders Name: Fangz.

# #6:LEAF-ERRS

They are average in height and small build. There specialty in combat is razor-sharp leaves, very small. There personality is very dry. They have no training. Leaders Name: Twigger.

# #7: SPRITE-ORRS

Same as the Leaf-Orr but different weapon. They are average in height and small build. There specialty in combat is spikes, very small. There personality is very dry. They have no training. Leaders Name: Brab.

# #8: ROCK-LORDS

Very huge build and very tall. There specialty in combat is maces and rocks. There personality is very close in being mute. They train off-n-on but can be determine. Leaders Name: Slice.

# #9: CANDY-POPS

Average height and weight. There specialty in combat is candy-canes. There personality is soft-spoken. They have no training at all. Leaders Name: Mittens.

# #10: TEA PARTY GANG

Very short and small. There specialty in combat is knives and very short swords. There personality is very stuck-up and very to-the-point in conversations. They have no training. Leaders Names: Top Hatz.

# CHAPTER 37

---

# REMAINING FOURTEEN ARMIES "WARRIOR JOB LIST"

Here are the fourteen "Warrior Job List". King Kraken only made them use certain skills to no else knows, only humans can perform them but they all have NO experience in combat. Some of these skills other species can perform like Archers and Squires. The rest are completely different to everyone else because it was never performed before. It was at a last moments notice, in the mind of King Kraken.

Here is the list but no information on them.

Soon will be a list to not be reckon with. They might not performed a great job in the great war but they will have their moment in history on this planet, Kraken.

"WARRIOR JOB LIST"
#1.Squire.
#2.Knight.

#3.Archer.
#4.Chemist.
#5.Monk.
#6.Black Mage.

#7.White Mage.
#8.Time Mage.
#9.Summoner.
#10.Geomancer.
#11.Thief.
#12.Lancer.
#13.Samurai.
#14.Ninja.

Princess Annie, Beard, Chainz and Malt saw the entire war between Lost Woods and King Kraken. These four souls, chosen ones or better yet four hopefuls of nature saw the great war in about four to five hours. But it seem it only taken twenty minutes because all four have awaken from the floor. The power from the crystal ball, in the mind, has taken a lot of time to see all of this but in reality, matter of minutes. As well, all the information collected from this little journey of the past, the twenty-nine armies, is from Princess Annie, Beard, Chainz and Malt of what they all saw and witnessed. In this world they were spirits, no one can't see or even touch them for that matter. Or they can't touch or feel anything. By walking around and gathering information on their own. Good experience if you ask me.

# FOUR SOULS OF NATURE

## NINE RINGS OF SOULS

# INTRO

In this third and final part of this story or for that matter, the conclusion of the whole series, takes place where Princess Annie, Beard, Chaniz and Malt wake up from the floor by the crystal ball that all four placed their hand on, received all the information about the twenty-nine armies and experienced it first-hand.

What will the second crystal ball reveal for our four wondering travelers? What will the plaque say in the description? Will all four come in contact with King Kraken or his pet Hydra? All these questions in this last part of this series and the answer to all of them is....press on forward and see what happens.

All things come to an end and last eternity. Princess Annie.......a character that will last for the ages to every specie out there. Will she finally crack a smile on her face? Will she find peace in her own mind? OR will she end up like King Scarecrow and King Iggy, live the rest of her life in guilt, sadness and alone in the darkness?

A series that will last forever if you think about it. Just like a storm, if you are in it, it will stay with you-in your own mind-FOREVER.

# CHAPTER 38

# SECOND CRYSTAL BALL

As all four woke up from the floor, next to the huge crystal ball, Princess Annie, Beard, Chainz and Malt all got up very slowly, shaking in fear.

Malt picked herself up, happen to find a bucket in the same room, started to throwing up her guts(her nerves were bad because of what she had witnessed in the past of the Great War).

Beard slowly got up and walked over to Malt and cried.

Chainz slowly got up as well, placed his two hands on his head and shaking left to right(he was trying to get that vision out of his head or should I say trying to use his mind to block it out).

Princess Annie got up slowly just like the others and walked over to the second crystal ball. A few seconds later she said, "That was fun. What do you three think of that little journey of the past? I know you all enjoyed it as much as I have, I know, I can see it in your eyes". With that said, Princess Annie threw up her guts, just like Malt have done.

After a while, the second crystal glowed black and a small beam came out of it, went into all four of the hopefuls head. Princess Annie, Beard, Chainz and Malt became well(in the mind). The beam ease-off what they all experienced but they all still remember it.

Beard, Chainz and Malt walked over to Princess Annie to join her by the other huge crystal ball, which is now glowing black, to where the beam came out. There was a plaque which in the past it was blank and now it reads "Nine Rings of Souls", with a description written on it, it reads......

"For the chosen ONE or chosen FOUR of all four elements-EARTH, FIRE, WATER and WIND-this will be in two different fields. If there is only one individual and not four, place your hand on the crystal ball and it will take you to the Nine Rings of Souls. But if it is foul individuals, all of you must decide which ONE will enter the Nine Rings of Souls. Four elements is too heavy, even for the afterlife. When you made a decision, placed your hand on the crystal ball".

P.S. "If it is four, whichever weapons that you are good at, that skill will go to that ONE and be able to use them in the Nine Rings of Souls. Plus three out of four of you will be absorb into the ONE entering the afterlife or should I say fuse together. Four single elements can not enter the afterlife only ONE with all FOUR elements into one can enter. If you succeed in this journey in the afterlife, the three that went into that ONE will be back as their own, just as you are now. Good luck"!

"Just like Iggy and Wormy of the past. They both fused together to form Igworm", said Princess Annie. Beard, Chainz and Malt did not comment of say a word.

# CHAPTER 39

# A DECISION IS MADE

Princess Annie, Beard, Chainz and Malt just looked over at each other after reading what was written on the plaque. "You guys decide but I am not going to the Nine Rings of Souls because I have no fighting experience, plus it did read that whoever goes down there will learn one another's ability to use whatever weapon they are good at, sorry", said Malt.

"Now it is down to three", said Beard. "I have the most out of the four", said Chainz. Princess Annie got out her small fan from her handbag again and started to waving it in her face. A few seconds later Princess Annie said, with her eye- brows raised, "This is just me but Malt is right, she has no experience, so true. Beard here is really weak physically but fast, according to your profile. Chainz here is really strong but very slow, according to his profile. I, myself is a mix of both plus I have use my blade, my weapon of warfare more times than Bread. Yes, Chainz has been in a few battles in his time but I think you are fed-up with fighting, yes? To think it is fair if I go th the Nine Rings of Souls and again I am not being rude and all".

"You have a point", said Beard. "And what do you know what I am thinking, Annabelle"? said Chainz, getting mad. "I don't know, I am just spitting out the facts", said Princess Annie. "My vote is Annabelle", said Malt. "Same here", said Beard. Chainz walked over to Princess Annie, patted her on the head and said, "I want my chains back". "So be it", said Princess Annie, with a small grin on her face.

She than placed her hand on the glowing black crystal ball. A few seconds later all three, Beard, Chainz and Malt flashed into a bright light and went inside Princess Annie (but did not change her appearance-so weird). A minute later, Princess Annie disappeared and the journey in the afterlife in the Nine Rings of Souls.....BEGINS!

# CHAPTER 40

# THE GUIDE IN THE NINE RINGS OF SOULS

Princess Annie entered into a realm of darkness, very quiet with no activity at all. A minute later a light appeared into a distance, so Princess Annie headed towards the light. Up ahead Princess Annie saw a figure standing next to the light.

"Hello Princess Annabelle Von Ada, Guardian of all Creatures", said the stranger, with a bow. "Who are you, mind me asking"? said Princess Annie. "My name is Ark-Wood, from the Insecta species. I will be your guide through the Nine Rings of Souls. Do not fear me child, I am here to help you and all you have to do is follow and listen to what I have to say, do you understand, Annabelle"? "Yes", said Princess Annie.

Ark-Wood handed Princess Annie a lantern. It glowed a dark bluish-white, the same color as Ark-Wood, he was covered all-over. Also Ark-Wood is male, not female because of his shape, size and somewhat tall as well.

"I have waited a long time for this moment Annabelle and he was right that it would be you to enter the Nine Rings of Souls and no it wasn't King Kraken who said it. When we reach the last ring, if everything goods well and smooth I will tell you who told me, I think that is fair", said Ark-Wood. "What are you"? said Princess Annie. "I used to be a poet in my time, in a continent called Heart-Grass and yes, it is from this planet of Kraken. But I also trained to fight as well", said Ark-Wood, as both pressed on forward to the first ring in the afterlife.

## CHAPTER 41

# RING #1-GUILT/ACTIONS OF PHYSICALLY

In the first ring of the Nine Rings of Souls, Princess Annie saw very large cubes with images of all different kinds of species engraved on them. The images looked like they were all being punished.

Ark-Wood hold up his staff and shined a bright light on these large cubes and a few seconds he said.....

"This first ring in this part of this realm in the Nine Rings Of Souls is called "Guilt/Actions of Physically". Which means that every possible species that lived here on this planet are being punished for their actions. They harm those alive of the flesh with not reason what-so-ever. They will not find peace or rest because of their guilt of what they all have committed. What they did up there, they feel the same amount of pain down here, ten-times more. These souls are trapped into these large cubes, never to be released, never to escape, never to find any hope at all".

Ark-Wood lower his staff and continued to walk down deeper in the Nine Rings of Souls. Princess Annie followed Ark-Wood down these open-wide spiral staircase. "I have a question for you Ark-Wood, how come my physical appearance did not change? Three of my traveling companions fuse into me"? Ark-Wood stop walking, turned around to look at Princess Annie and said, "Time will tell, no more questions please".

# CHAPTER 42

---

# RING #2-GUILT/ACTIONS OF MENTALLY

In the second ring of the Nine Rings of Souls, Princess Annie saw very large cubes....again, but they were different this time. They were covered in a mist and different cravings engraved on them all. It looked like faces of all kinds of species, with their hands placed on another ones head, like a chain-like image, everyone was doing it. Ark-Wood hold up his staff and shined a bright light on these cubes and said.....

> "This second ring in this part of this realm in the afterlife is called "Guilt/Actions of Mentally". Here is the species of all kinds that tormented, harassed, threatened, and yes, even bullied those alive for no reason and even gave themselves pleasure for it all. They attacked those innocent in the mind. The mind is more fragile than the body, that is why it is more offending than physical. In time their souls will incinerate in ashes because the guilt

is such a powerful tool on a individual. They age quick, change of skin and also the crumbling in their voices too".

Ark-Wood lower his staff and continued on his way to the third ring in the Nine Rings of Souls, along with Princess Annie, going deeper into the afterlife.

# CHAPTER 43

---

# RING#3-GUILT/NO ACTION

In the third ring of the Nine Rings of Souls, Princess Annie saw cubes again but they were all different. The cubes were covered in skulls of all kinds of species(different size of the skull) and the image on the cubes looked like different species sitting down, doing nothing. Ark-Wood hold up his staff and shined a bright light on these large cubes and said......

"This third ring in this part of this realm in the afterlife is called "Guilt-No Action". This ring is far more worse than physical or mental. These souls which at one point alive, did not take action for no one or better yet cowards-did not defend the innocent, only watch, sitting back and smiling. Never help out no one else only please themselves. For example, if they saw someone get bullied or being punched for no reason, they would just stand there pleasing themselves, in their on mind, being entertained, drinking and smoking. No rest indeed for these cowards, no rest until their soul is completely turn to ashes and that would be the only time they would feel no pain".

Ark-Wood lower his staff and continued on his way but not to the fourth ring in the Nine Rings of Souls but on the same level. Up ahead was a door, with a Hydra engraved in it. Both Ark-Wood and Princess Annie went in and at this point, things will start to "change" for Princess Annie.

# CHAPTER 44

---

# CREATORS CREATION #1/HYDRA

"Here is the spirit of the Hydra, King Krakens first specie he has created using the sinful souls right here in the Nine Rings of Souls. In order to press-on forward you have to defeat this Hydra in combat. If you fail, you will go back to your regular life and King Kraken is reborn, which is something we don't want. You will understand, trust me Annabelle. To help you, I will give you a shield, handed down with our ancestors of the Insecta's. I will wait outside and good luck", said Ark-Wood.

Ark-Wood raised his staff and it glowed a dark blue. Suddenly a shield appeared right in front of Princess Annie. Seconds later Ark-Wood walked out the the door and closing it behind him.

About a minute later, the spirit of the Hydra appeared in front of Princess Annie, in a distance. The spirit revealed itself the same image back at the Sealed Kingdom. Princess Annie picked up the shield and ready her long sword. The

Hydra was a bit fast but no arms and legs, like a snake. Next thing the Hydra breathe out some bluish-fire in a distance. Princess Annie said to herself, in a low tone of voice, "When this Hydra breathes fire at me, I will charge at him with this shield and smash the shield in the face than take my long sword and drive it up through him, bottom-up from his mouth. When he goes to breathe fire at me again, he will only incinerate his insides because he can't open his month".

And it work. Princess Annie did all of this of what she said and the Hydra was nothing but ashes at the end of the day. "That should put some flavor in your mouth", said Princess Annie. After Princess Annie left the room to go to meet up with Ark-Wood.

"I am not surprised, not one bit. Just to let you know you have three more duels left plus a reward after each victory. The prizes are Chainz weapon-chains, Beards bow-n-arrows and Malts height. And yes I know these three souls are inside you and I will explain everything to you at the last ring, if you make it that far, time will tell, my child. So which award do you want"? said Ark-Wood. "I want the ability to use chains", said Princess Annie. "So be it", said Ark-Wood. He raised up his staff and shined a beam of light at Princess Annie. Next thing, wrapped around her long sword, are a nice pair of chains. Light as a feather, very long and very flexible too.

"Ok! Off to the next ring, shall we"? said Ark-Wood, leading the way. As Princess Annie followed, she felt stronger with every step she has taken, with a small little grin on her face to go with it too.

# CHAPTER 45

---

# RING #4-EARTH ELEMENT

In the fourth ring of the Nine Rings of Souls, Princess Annie is very proud to have the gift to use chains in combat, saw a huge chest there in a dark brown color but no images engraved on it. Ark-Wood hold up his staff and shined a bright light from it and said......

"This fourth ring in this part of this realm in the afterlife is housing the element-EARTH. The reason why this element is here in the Nine Rings of Souls is because the species up above covered the grounds with blood-out of violence, greed, power and the list goes on. They even use earth from the ground to create evil like the Grave Diggers, Iggy's and Wormy's, they are a prime example of it. Also the Tree-Elk species, they need earth to plant their roots into the ground to stay healthy and strong, were all killed off except for one because of their height, power and knowledge-how sad if you ask me".

"Ark-Wood lower his staff and continued on his way to the fifth ring in the Nine Rings of Souls. Princess Annie followed and said to herself in a low tone of voice, "Is it me or am I not scared. I am not even shaking. Could be the power of the fusing-strange indeed".

# CHAPTER 46

---

# RING #5-FIRE ELEMENT

In the fifth ring of the Nine Rings of Souls, Princess Annie saw another huge chest but this time in a dark red color with no images on it engraved. Ark-Wood hold up his staff and shined a bright light from it and said.....

"This fifth ring in this part of this realm in the afterlife is housing the element-FIRE. The reason why this element is here in the Nine Rings of Souls is because of the species anger and jealously of others. With this much tension, it is the same as fire, it never rests until you put in out with water. Fire itself killed a lot of species too. Like the Tree-Elk species, while others were tortured to death with this element. You see fire is also used to make weapons, tools of war, if you want to call it. Melting metal and changing the shape to make different kinds of items and not just weapons either, like walls and fences. If fire could be controlled like someone else's anger, for example, than you don't need to have buckets of water as a stand-by just in case if that fire spreads".

Ark-Wood lower his staff and continued on his way to the sixth ring in the Nine Rings of Souls. Princess Annie followed, shaking her head left to right, saying to herself in a low tone of voice, "Why me, why me"?

# CHAPTER 47

---

# RING #6-WIND ELEMENT

In the sixth ring of the Nine Rings of Souls, Princess Annie again saw another huge chest there in a white color and no images on it engraved. Ark-Wood hold up his staff and shined a bright light from it and said......

"This sixth ring in this part of this realm in the afterlife is housing the element-WIND. The reason why this element is here in the Nine Rings of Souls is because it cannot be controlled. It is everywhere-makes sandstorms from the earth, makes the fire spread faster and goes on stronger plus it also makes tidal waves in the oceans. Just like emotions, thinking up plans in life or better yet the thought of taking a life away. It is everywhere, negativity, mostly in the mind. I go by the MEDIUM which stands for: M-Mind Reading, E-Extreme Thinking, D-Dwelling on the Negative, I-Ignoring the Positive, U-Unfounded Conclusions, M-Misfortunate Telling. If there was no wind at all, this world would be at ease and maybe a better place in the past".

Ark-Wood lower his staff and continued to the seventh ring in the Nine Rings of Souls. Following right behind Ark-Wood, Princess Annie did what she was told. Not ask any questions and go with the "flow", like wind.

## CHAPTER 48

---

# RING #7-WATER ELEMENT

In the seventh ring of the Nine Rings of Souls, Princess Annie saw her fourth huge chest in a different color. It was in a dark blue color and with no images engraved on it either. Ark-Wood hold up his staff and shined a bright light from it and said........

"This seventh ring in this part of this realm in the afterlife is housing the element-WATER. The reason why this element is here in the Nine Rings of Souls is because everyone, species of all kinds, filled this planet up with tears, sadness, despair and even no hope. Water can swallow the earth, fire and even wind. It is the heavens above make the rain that make this element the deadest of the four. Not only nature but to species, it is more-less out of fear. You see, fear is used for either good or bad when you "think" about it just like water-you water plants OR you drown them-hard to tell with that element now-a-days".

Ark-Wood lower his staff and continued on his way yet to another door on the same level of the seventh ring in the Nine Rings of Souls. The door was engraved with a Grave Digger on it. Ark-Wood and Princess Annie went into the room and another duel was about to begin for the Guardian of the Creatures.

# CHAPTER 49

## CREATORS CREATIONS #2 GRAVE DIGGER MINION

"Here is the spirit of a Grave Digger minion, King Krakens second species he has created using the sinful souls right here in the Nine Rings of Souls. Just like before, you have to defeat this minion in order to progress Princess Annie. If you win, you will be rewarded with either the bow-n-arrows OR increase your height to five-foot-five. Right now you are master with the chains. Good luck and I will see you outside if you prevail".

With that Ark-Wood walked out of the room, closing the door behind him.

About a minute later, the spirit of a Grave Digger minion appeared in front of Princess Annie. "What a privilege it is to be in front of you but I have to end you, sorry", said Princess Annie. With that said, Princess Annie flung out her chains and snatched the Grave Diggers sword. With no sword at hand, the Grave Digger ran towards Princess Annie. "You want your sword back, here, take it", said Princess Annie. So she threw the sword back at the Grave Digger with her chains and struck him right in the belly. He fell down and Princess Annie went over, lifted her leg up and knocked the sword deeper into his belly, the Grave Digger is dead... disappeared into thin air.

Princess Annie walked out the room, close the door behind her and greeted Ark-Wood. "Well done child. Now which will it be, bow-n-arrows OR height"? said Ark-Wood. "Height"! said Princess Annie. "So be it", said Ark-Wood .With that, Ark-Wood raised his staff and a bright light came out of it and went in Princess Annie. She was no longer three-foot-ten but five-foot-five. "Off to the next ring", said Ark-Wood.

## CHAPTER 50

# RING #8-HALF SQUID/HALF CREATURE

In the eighth ring of the Nine Rings of Souls, Princess Annie saw a huge casket with a creature engraved on it that she saw before she entered the grounds of the Sealed Kingdom, the half squid/ half creature. Ark-Wood hold up his staff and shined a bright light from it and said.....

"This eighth ring in this part of this realm in the afterlife is where the half squid/half creature rests. What a specie it is indeed but very deadly, dangerous and a seed that was planted with the wrong materials. At one time this creature WAS the first to be here on this planet before King Kraken arrived here. Very evil-no regard to life at all but what makes this type of species interesting is that it knew what he was doing like this planet, he destroyed everything here, all that was left was rock and soil. His weapon is spitting out a black substance, looks like oil and very poisonous too. The Father cast him out of his realm because the specie wanted to control the Divine World. After what the specie did to the planet, the Father destroyed the half squid/half creature, in polite terms, giving the specie a second chance at life, just like King Kraken. The Father-I will tell you if you reach the last ring, ok? The specie here will remain in the eighth ring in the afterlife of the Nine Rings of Souls for all eternity, in his torment for going against the Father".

Ark-Wood lower his staff and continued on his way yet to another door on the same level of the eighth ring in the Nine Rings of Souls. The door was engraved with a Iggy minion on it. Ark-Wood and Princess Annie went into the room and a third duel was about to begin for Annabelle Von Ada.

# CHAPTER 51

# CREATORS CREATIONS #3/IGGY MINION

"Here is the spirit of a Iggy minion, King Krakens third specie he has created using the sinful souls right here in the Nine Rings of Souls. If you defeat this spirit, you will be rewarded with the bow-n-arrows Princess Annie. And again if you lose, well, you know what will happen. Good luck and I will see you outside if you gain victory".

Ark-Wood headed towards the door, opened it and walked out, closing the door behind him.

About a minute later, the spirit of a Iggy minion appeared in front of Princess Annie. "So you are the one-half of Igworm. I have to say, you are more ugly in person than what is written in the history books back at the Mermen keep", said Princess Annie. With that said, the Iggy minion ran towards Princess Annie at great speed. Princess Annie threw her chains at the Iggy minion, tripped and tied his legs together with his sword out of his hands. Princess Annie walked over the Iggy Minion, got her long sword out and cut the head off clean from his shoulders-the Iggy minion is dead-disappeared into thin air.

Princess Annie walked out the room, closed the door behind her to meet her guide in the Nine Rings of Souls-Ark-Wood. "And again well done Annabelle. Here is your reward, you have earn it or should I say-all three of them", said Ark-Wood. With that said, Ark-Wood hold up his staff and a bright light came out of it and went into Princess Annie. On her back was a bow-n-arrows into one.

Finally we are going to the last ring", said Ark-Wood. Princess Annie followed but this time with a big grin on her face.

## CHAPTER 52

# RING #9-FAREWELL TO ARK-WOOD

In the ninth and final ring in the Nine Rings of Souls, Princess Annie didn't realize how deep she and Ark-Wood have traveled into the world of the afterlife of the sins the species committed. "We are almost there child. It is a little deeper this time but I will not go any further", said Ark-Wood.

"Why"? said Princess Annie. "Because I was told by the Father, the true creator of the Divine World and also this planet. You will meet not one but two individuals there. One is King Krakens fourth and final spirit he has created using the sinful souls right here in the Nine Rings of Soul-the Wormy minion. Second, King Kraken himself will be there. If you defeat the Wormy minion, I will give you another special gift, it is a surprise, NOW GO", said Ark-Wood.

"Master, will we meet again"? said Princess Annie, with a few tears rolled down her face. "Child, ready yourself for the two final encounters. Do not think of me, if you prevail-I will see you on the other side", said Ark-Wood, with a bow. With that said, Ark-Wood disappeared.

Princess Annie, with her lantern at hand, followed the open-wide spiral staircase until she came to a very huge door with a Wormy minion engraved on it. "I guess it is time to face the second-half of Igworm", said Princess Annie. She opened the door, went in and closed it behind her.

# CHAPTER 53

---

# CREATORS CREATION #4/WORMY MINION

Standing in front of Princess Annie, in a distance, is a Wormy minion. "This is interesting, were you waiting for me? How polite and nice of you to do that", said Princess Annie. Just like the Grave Digger and Iggy minion, the Wormy minion charged at Princess Annie, armed with a sword and shield at hand.

Princess Annie first got out her bow-n-arrows and fired at the Wormy minions legs and feet, he went down on one knee. Second, Princess Annie threw her chains at the Wormy minion's sword, grabbed it and threw it to the other side of the room and with no sword at hand for the Wormy minion. Third, Princess Annie threw her shield at the Wormy minion's shield and knock it out of his hand. Completely defenseless, the Wormy minion hopped towards Princess Annie. "Give me a break", said Princess

Annie, as she got out her bow-n-arrows out again, fired a few more at his legs until he fell down, face-first. When the Wormy minion lifted his head up to look at Princess Annie, she fired an arrow and struck him between the eyes-the Wormy minion is dead-disappeared into thin air.

Suddenly one of the walls in the same room turned into a door with an image of King Kraken engraved in it. After that happen, Princess Annie's clothes turned into armor-it felt light and very strong at the same time, with a helmet and silver boots-all silver all-over. "Thank-you Ark-Wood", said Princess Annie.

After all this happen, Princess Annie opened the door, enter the room and closed the door behind her.

# CHAPTER 54

---

# CREATORS CASKET OPENS

In this room, very cold and damp, it had to be the blackest, saddest, depressing looking part of the Nine Rings of Souls. In the middle of this room was a very large silver casket. Princess Annie walked over to the casket, with her lantern at hand(without this lantern, she probably could not see where she was going). A plaque was there with a description written on it, it reads......

> "Here lies my son, King Kraken, who will be forever missed. His power got the best of him, went to his head if you want to call it. I did not banish him not like that half squid/half creature. If Kraken had proper training and better counseling, maybe this world would be a safer place. I cast him out of the Divine World, an eye-sore at that time. I did not what to do this but I had very little choice. Maybe Kraken will understand one day and I hope the chosen ONE will help him, If not then the chosen

ONE will have my permission to rid his evil-thinking-FOREVER-and spend the rest of his eternity here in the Nine Rings of Souls".

*Jehovah, Father And Creator Of The Divine World*

After reading what was on the plaque, the casket started to open. Princess Annie stepped back quickly. "I was waiting for you, Annabelle Von Ada", said a voice from the casket. A minute later, standing up inside the large silver casket and a figure that Princess Annie have seen before, King Kraken turn around to look at Princess Annie, with a glare that could even kill the dead itself.

# CHAPTER 55

---

# KING KRAKEN CONFRONTS PRINCESS ANNIE

"You have released me from this realm of the Nine Rings of Souls, thank-you Annabelle Von Ada. Before you say anything I will do the talking and you will have your say, fair"! said King Kraken.

King Kraken got out of the casket, walked around for about a minute and turned around to look over at Princess Annie and said with a grin on his face, "Where do I start, oh yes, I will start with Scarecrow. I planned for Scarecrow to have the gift to make many kind of weapons in the world like the "Warrior Job List". I sent parts of my soul in the afterlife BEFORE I was put in imprisonment in this cursed casket. The "Flame of Creation" I have created in the afterlife with the sinful souls help and make out that Hope and the other pure-innocent souls created it. Poor Queen Sandra- made it look it was her fault and it wasn't-genius".

King Kraken took a breather and continued, "The sword "Flame of Creation", is made from the four elements right here in the Nine Rings of Souls-EARTH, created the Hydra-Grave Diggers-Iggy's-Wormy's. WATER, mix it with the soil and rocks. FIRE, give them all life from the heat. WIND, spread them out like a wild fire, make multiples of them. The Hydra was my escape but YOU killed him-not bad. And all of these plans failed but YOU are the ONE with all four elements. Your element is WATER, when you fused with the other three, you gained them all".

King Kraken gave Princess Annie a big smile, "And my daughter, Annabelle Von Ada. My soul went into your mother, Veronica Card, before said married Felix Von Ada. I did the same to Jeremy Andrews, his mother Amber, before she got married".

"One last thing Annabelle Von Ada, the "Flame of Creation" and the half squid/half creature, I FUSED them into one. I released the swords power when King Scarecrow died of old age. That half squid/half creature in the eighth ring was Wormy and from the "Flame of Creation" was Iggy, in disguise as a creature. So what do you think of my hard work, Annabelle Von Ada"? said King Kraken.

Princess Annie walked closer to King Kraken and said, "I have to hand it to you FATHER, you are not as stupid as I thought. But you forgot one thing. I am not like you and you have failed.... AGAIN". "Really? Tell me Annabelle, if I failed than how come I am released from this casket? My creations set me free and you did that.....sorry but my soul is in you too", said King Kraken. "You created SIX not

FOUR=Hydra, Grave Diggers, Iggy's, Wormy's, Scarecrow and myself. You have fouled a lot of people and species alike.....that's good. But you forgot one thing, a small miss in your calculations", said Princess Annie, "And what is that"? said King Kraken. "If I die NOW, so do you because you are free. This casket here was protecting you and now you are out, you are variable to man and woman alike. Just think about it, every piece of your soul is destroyed but mine", said Princess Annie. With that said, King Kraken lost his grin.

# CHAPTER 56

# R.I.P. KING KRAKEN

"You wouldn't hurt your dear daughter, would you, FATHER"? said Princess Annie. King Kraken did not comment. "If I kill you Kraken, I win. But if you kill me, you will be killing the last piece of your soul-ME-than I will still win and you will die. Boy are you stupid, no knowledge or wisdom at all and Lost Woods was right about that too", said Princess Annie.

Princess Annie got out her long sword and started to walk towards King Kraken. "Listen I am a change man, you have to believe me. Just look at the Sealed Kingdom, both outside and inside, I showed my love for the fallen. Listen well child, how about you and I worked together. I created you to help me take down Jehovah, it is all his fault, you have to believe me", said King Kraken, getting nervous and sweating a lot right now. "It is not going to happen, KING"? said Princess Annie. With that Princess Annie's long sword glowed in different colors, she raised it up and fired a beam from it. It struck King Kraken at all different parts of his body.

King Kraken screamed in pain, the body turning into ashes and his soul went back inside the casket. Under the casket, large roots wrapped the casket all around and the whole thing went underground. A second later, Princess Annie's body glowed a dark blue, the soul came out of her, it was King Kraken. Less than a second, he screamed and went underground to join the rest of his remains of his sad, depressing, weak soul for all eternity, along with the roots that drag him there.

# CHAPTER 57

# JEHOVAH APPEARS

"Kraken wasn't the most intelligent individual but at the end of the day, he DID foul me". said a voice in a distance. "Who is it? Who are you"? said Princess Annie, with her long sword ready in her hand.

A graceful figure approached from a distance, very tall, white robe, long white hair mixed with grey, and his beard very long as well. "My name is Jehovah and you must be Annabelle Von Ada, the chosen ONE. I don't mean to be rude but you are Kraken's failed experiment or should I say a seed that never ripen'. "I take that as an accomplishment-thank", said Princess Annie, with a small grin on her face.

Jehovah went over to Princess Annie and gave her a big hug and a kiss on each side of her face.

Princess Annie cried and wiped the tears with her arm. "I am very proud of you Annabelle Von Ada. All the souls were used to make the species that Kraken has made here in the Nine Rings of Souls will get their name cleared. Kraken promised them all a new life, a new beginning but only used them all BEFORE he was cast in this casket I have made for him", said Jehovah.

Princess Annie got a breather in and said,"Were you the spirit that came to me in my bedroom that night"? "NO, that was not me, it was your guide-Ark-Wood. He was the first and ONLY one to enter my realm-ALIVE- because of his faith and passion on nature plus he is a very good poet in writing sayings, just like you did", said Jehovah. "You made a wise choice", said Princess Annie, smiling.

# CHAPTER 58

# JEHOVAH GIVE PRINCESS ANNIE THE ULTIMATE REWARD

"**N**ow I have a reward for you Annabelle Von Ada. Here is a list and you can only pick ONE. Take your time-no rush", said Jehovah. Out of his white robe, Jehovah handed Princess Annie a scroll and here is what is written on it, it reads......

*"Nine choices only one prevails, choose one for yourself, a gift from the Father of the Divine World"*

#1: Go back to the same life-Sealed Kingdom disappears.

#2: Sealed Kingdom rises and a new ruler is needed.

#3: Sealed Kingdom disappears and every specie reborn from the Great War-chosen ONE goes to Divine World.

#4: Chosen ONE, Beard, Chainz and Malt have element power-only one will rule the Sealed Kingdom underground.

#5: This planet will start from scratch and the chosen ONE will make a new world.

#6: Reborn the fake Scarecrow and Igworm

again-reunite every specie only from the Great War to battle these foes to re-gain their honor.

#7: Beard, Chainz and Malt will live in the Sealed Kingdom underground-ruled by the creatures- chosen ONE goes to the Divine World.

#8: Beard, Chainz and Malt will live in the Sealed Kingdom-it will rise from the ground-ruled by the Mermen-chosen ONE goes the Divine World.

#9: Create new life-absorb the Sealed Kingdoms power-live with the species-ruler of the planet- rename the planet.


P.S. "You can only leave the Nine Rings of Souls when you make a decision.


*Jehovah, Ruler And Creator Of The Divine World*

# CHAPTER 59

# PRINCESS ANNIE'S DECISION

"So many choices to choose from, what do you think Jehovah? Which one out of the nine would you choose"? said Princess Annie. "I can't help you Annabelle and I am not being rude. Also it does not matter which one I would have pick, really", said Jehovah. "Whichever one I choose, I want you to tell me which one you would have picked, fair? It is just between us, ok"? said Princess Annie. "Fair"! said Jehovah.

Princess Annie walked around for a bit and said, "#7 and #8 choices would come to a point if possible war between the creatures and the Mermen. #6 choice would be an eye-sore plus no one what's another war, period. #5 choice that the planet is hurt with the memories of the past, this planet will get better as long every specie shows the planet so comfort, so why destroy it and make a new world? #4 choice, to me, its very possible that the power of an element would got to someone's head".

"Which leaves to only four choices left", said Jehovah. "Yes"! said Princess Annie, "I really need a change in nature so #1 choice is off the list. The Sealed Kingdom, to me, is another eye-sore, it should disappear. I know it has good memories of the species but that memory is too great so #2 choice is out, which leaves me with #3 and #9 choices left".

"So which one out of the two Annabelle that you want that is pleasing to you"? said Jehovah.

Princess Annie walked around for a bit, turned around to look at Jehovah, with a few tears run down her face, "The one I have chosen is number......"

"Great choice indeed Annabelle Von Ada. The one I would have chosen is number......"

# CHAPTER 60

---

# MEANWHILE . . . . .

A young group of children, between the ages of eight to twelve, were headed to the gloomy, wooden realm on this planet-Lost Woods. Four to be exact. Two creatures-boy and a girl, a merman-boy and a human-boy. "I saw her headed towards Lost Woods", said the girl creature. "By herself, no way", said the boy. "Well, she is trained by the Mermen". said the merman boy. "She even disguised herself as well", said the boy creature.

As all four entered Lost Woods and reached to the memorial site of the Cherry Blossom tree and the village that used to house a group of creatures in the past, the girl creature placed a small basket of strawberries by the Cherry Blossom tree.

"I don't know why you creatures do all this for Princess Annie, she doesn't even care about you", said the boy. "She does too", said the girl creature. "It is hard to know these days", said the merman boy. "Plus she never smiles so....", said the boy creature.

"What makes you all think I don't care about you all", said a voice in the woods. "Who said that"? said the boy. Out of the woods walking gracefully, stood Princess Annie, wearing silk green clothing all-over. "She is not wearing black", said the boy. "She is smiling", said the boy creature. "She is tall", said the merman boy. "She is here because she likes.....strawberries", said the girl creature.

"It is me, Princess Annie and don't be afraid. After all, everyone needs changing, yes"? said Princess Annie. All four children just stared at her puzzled, confused and..... happy to see Princess Annie smiling.

# CHAPTER 61

---

# FRESH NEW START

Princess Annie left Lost Woods along with four wondering children-out of concern for the Guardian of all Creatures and the one who used to dress in black when she became "Princess".

Along the way home, around 9:50 P.M. in the evening(the whole adventure started in the morning and ending in the evening-on the same day-go figure), all five were greeted by a couple of Gob-wings. Princess Annie said the Gob-wings, "With your permission, can you give these young fine protectors here a ride home, including myself, we are all very tired, please. Thank-you all for coming out to see how I am, I really appreciate it plus I have something to tell everyone - Kingdom of Hope, Kingdom of Hydra and the head of the Mermen at the keep in the mountains. Tomorrow we will all celebrate and everyone is invited", said Princess Annie, smiling.

Back at Princess Annie's cottage/tree house keep, about three creatures saw Princess Annie in a distance, in complete shock, "She is tall", said one creature. "She is smiling", said another creature. "She is wearing green and not black....it is a sign", said the third creature. About a few minutes later Princess Annie greeted the three creatures standing outside, "Sorry to worry all of you, how are things? Big news tomorrow and a big celebration too".

Around 10:35 P.M. at night, just as Princess Annie was all cleaned up and ready to go to bed, a knock was at the bedroom door, "Come in", said Princess Annie. "A creature came in(the same one that spoken to Princess Annie last night), "How was your journey outside"? Princess Annie turned around to look at the creature and said, "It was quite......educational. I think that is the polite terms of this journey. I am tired and thank-you for looking after my keep, I really appreciate it, goodnight". "And you as well", said the creature, closing the door behind him.

# CHAPTER 62

---

# NEW MEMBERS OF THE FAMILY

Around 7:00 A.M. in the morning, which is on a Saturday, Princess Annie got out of bed, washed-up, got dressed, made the bed and headed downstairs. Before any of the creatures said anything to Princess Annie, she has spoken first, "Today is going to be a brand-new beginning for everyone and so much to tell everyone. We will start first just outside. We will set-up tables and chairs, lots of food to go around plus drinks as well. And yes, I would like a small breakfast thank- you because you were going to ask me anyway, not be rude and all".

"Plus we are going to have new members to the family to join us humans, creatures, Mermen, the Gob-wings and the Father too", said Princess Annie. "Who is this Father? What new members"? said one of the creatures. "The Father will be a special guest here tonight and his name is Jehovah. The new members of the family are called Cherry Blossoms, like the ones on that big white tree in Lost Woods. They are a plant-like species, short but some are average height with arms and leg, of course. But they will look like a cherry blossom flower-they are not made or created yet- I am going to create them with the Sealed Kingdoms power. And I will tell you about the Sealed Kingdom to- night to everyone-don't worry", said Princess Annie, smiling(for the first longest time in her life).

# CHAPTER 63

---

# HISTORY . . . . . LEGEND

Here is a break-down of what happen down the years. Princess Annie was given a new title and crown, "Queen Annabelle Von Ada-Guardian to all species on the planet Sin-Free". Why this name for the planet-because the souls in the Nine Rings of Souls are free from their sins except the half squid/half creature. And yes, even King Kraken got forgiveness from his Father-Jehovah.

The cherry blossoms came to life by all the souls in the Nine Rings of Souls-pure as water. They build a huge castle, with lots of help from everyone-including the Gob-wings (most of the time they would just please themselves). The castle look almost exactly like the Sealed Kingdom (maybe the souls in the cherry blossoms wanted it that way- who knows). Also they all gave it a name-Kingdom of Lost Woods-good catch I think.

Beard, Chainz and Malt- they all went to the Divine World, Queen Annabelle insisted it because she said they all helped her in the Nine Rings of Souls-Beards bow-n-arrows, Chainz chains and Malts height. Jehovah granted it on the behalf of Queen Annabelle.

Queen Annabelle-she remained at her cottage/tree house keep. She married a gardener named Bernard and she gave birth to two children, a boy named Victor and a girl named Tina. Plus she ask the creatures to make her keep a bit bigger because they needed more room. Queen Annabelle lived a good, healthy life at a good age of ninety-three years of age. Her son's son was the next king of the planet of Sin-Free (the rule states that it had to be a young male or female of the first born which means a young off-spring from an older off-spring of Queen Annabelle, and if there was no young off-spring, they goes to the next old offspring to see they have made any children). Queen Annabelle went to the Divine World to join the others after her passing. As well, everyone species alive made statutes in her image to be remember for all time plus every specie written books about her as well.

This concludes the whole series-FOREVER!


THE END-FOR ALL ETERNITY!

# CHAPTER 59

"Are you surprised I have chosen #9"? said Princess Annie. "A bit but I thought you were going to pick either choice #8 or choice #2, guess I was wrong", said Jehovah. "The choice you have chosen, I am surprised indeed", said Princess Annie. "You mean choice #4. Well, all four of you are a symbol of it-Beard is EARTH, Chainz is FIRE, Malt is WIND and you, Annabelle, is WATER- makes sense but you gave your reasons for each choice so I guess all of that makes the most sense", said Jehovah.

"I have a question-where did Kraken get this "Warrior Job List", mind me asking", said Princess Annie. "He stole the list from me, that is the main reason why I cast him out of my realm. Stealing someone else's work and absorbing it into their mind forever-very dangerous I think", said Jehovah.

"I guess I don't need this armor Ark-Wood gave me or for that matter the bow-n-arrows, chains, shield and Malts height", said Princess Annie. Jehovah stared at Princess

Annie for a few seconds and later said, "Your armor will be silk green clothing, you will keep your new height as well. As for the bow-n-arrows, chains and shield...... well......I will hang on to them. I will give the shield to the Mermen, the chains to the creatures and the bow-n-arrows to the humans, or should I say in order-Mermen's Keep, Kingdom of Hope and the Kingdom of Hydra- as a token of peace". "Sounds good", said Princess Annie.

"As for Beard, Chainz and Malt-they will live in my realm forever-they deserve that. After all they had a part in the Nine Rings of Souls, you have used their tools of war. Plus I will drop by at your keep, yourself and I will everyone what has happen down here.....the Sealed Kingdom...... EVERYTHING", said Jehovah.

"Except for the choice you would have pick for yourself", said Princess Annie, grinning after saying that. "Exactly", said Jehovah. "Before I leave Jehovah, one more question and this will be the last one, I promise", said Princess Annie. "And what question do you have in mind Annabelle" said Jehovah. "Who named the Kingdom of Hydra-"HYDRA", do you know"? "I am a smart man Annabelle but I think the Mermen knew about King Krakens pet, even thought he created this beast in the Nine Rings of Souls. Maybe he has spoken to the Mermen AFTER the war. King Kraken wasn't send right away in the afterlife-I gave him time to think of what he has done, that is when he decided to divide his souls into different pieces-SIX to be exact. Plus he can even go to the afterlife as he pleased because he can sent parts of his soul down there. I created the Nine Rings of

Souls-not Kraken. Enough talk-off you go", said Jehovah. A few seconds later Princess Annie, with tears roll down her face, disappeared from the afterlife, out of the Nine Rings of Souls.

About a minute later, Jehovah said to himself, "If Annabelle found out the truth, she would never be the same. If Annabelle Von Ada knew SHE was the half squid/half creature in the past, probably none of this would not happen. And she was just a child when she fused with a seed she created-all hell broke loose-thanks to that son of mine Kraken. Her soul was in that creature, Kraken used part of his soul and went into Annabelle's soul-to make one complete soul, dumb boy. If she dies, he dies and she still lives. Because he cheated the system in the afterlife-one soul for one-not in six different bodies", said Jehovah.

Jehovah looked over to where the casket was that held his son Kraken and said, "Annabelle Von Ada will NEVER know her past-her true past-she deserves that........I think".

# EXTRAS

# ARK-WOOD'S SHORT SAYINGS

#1:    Fear the Father, he will reward you ten times more!

#2:    Come unto thee with help, it will be remembered for eternity!

#3:    Blessed are those who are thankful, for the end is not the end!

#4:    Why harm nature? Are they that beautiful?

#5:    Everybody pities the weak, jealously you have to earn!

#6:    Why me? Why such a gift? Am I that "fruitful" to the Father?

#7:    Individuals remember good deeds, while others remember the "thought" of helping.

#8:    Harm unto thee-no peace, help unto thee-no thanks, please yourself unto one soul-no sleep, no thanks, no peace!

#9:    Take pictures of nature unto them-no freedom in the mind!

#10:   Innocent things-boring, guilty things-adventure!

#11:   See no evil-hear no evil-means "sinless"?

#12:   The hand holds and the feet walks, the mind-endless!

#13:   Good shape-recognize, out-of-shape-not recognize.
       Where does "average" belong in?

#14:   Good fences make good neighbors-really?
       Fences can block out even one-persons opinion?-interesting!

#15:   Freedom of speech-does that mean whatever you say goes?

#16:   Mirrors-are they really "reflecting" the truth on ones individuals personality or are they really "breaking" the truth on one individuals thinking, a scary "image" if you ask me!

#17: Drink unto another individuals drink-talked.
Drink unto thy self-silence. "Talk" in "silence" is the best drink.

#18: If you don't see anyone in a long time, does that mean they are "busy" or does it mean they are just "passing by" in the neighbor!

#19: Baskets hold fruit, buckets hold water-which one is stronger? Baskets or Buckets? They both hold the same but it is the individual who carries them!

#20: If you believe in one, you have to believe there are two.
Two is one-one is two!

#21: Individuals say others look better dead than alive-true?

#22: Travel unto one-self see more. Travel unto them-see less!

#23: Ranks-does this mean they "earn" them?

#24: Happy is one, happy is more-means sadness all over!

#25: Dolls-great listeners. Others-great mind blocker's!

#26: Paint unto you-true self, paint unto them-illusion!

#27: Booze-cures sadness for a brief moment in time, winning-cures happiness for a brief moment in time. Which one can an individual "drink" for "pleasure"?

#28: Do clocks really tell us the "time" in our life?

#29: He gave me food- will not starve, he gave me drink-will not thirst, he gave me life-take it away or live it?

#30: Hot or cold-no win situation!

#31: Every writer as a beginning-will it end in writing?

#32: An apple-the first fruit in the beginning, will it be the end or will another fruit take its place and be "that"end?

#33: Are famous individuals important? Or is it their "issues" that make them all "famous"?

# Ark-Wood
*Species of the Insectas and Disciple of Jehovah*
*Father of the Divine World*

www.ingramcontent.com/pod-product-compliance
Lightning Source LLC
Chambersburg PA
CBHW020308150626
46552CB00022B/2093